THE MARVELOUS LAND OF OZ

VOL. 1

ADAPTED FROM THE NOVEL BY L. FRANK BAUM

Writer: **ERIC SHANOWER**
Artist: **SKOTTIE YOUNG**
Colorist: **JEAN-FRANCOIS BEAULIEU**
Letterer: **JEFF ECKLEBERRY**

Assistant Editor: **MICHAEL HORWITZ**
Editor: **NATE COSBY**

Collection Editor: **MARK D. BEAZLEY**
Assistant Editors: **ALEX STARBUCK & NELSON RIBEIRO**
Editor, Special Projects: **JENNIFER GRÜNWALD**
Senior Editor, Special Projects: **JEFF YOUNGQUIST**
SVP of Print & Digital Publishing Sales: **DAVID GABRIEL**
Production: **JERRY KALINOWSKI**
Book Design: **ARLENE SO**

Editor in Chief: **AXEL ALONSO**
Chief Creative Officer: **JOE QUESADA**
Publisher: **DAN BUCKLEY**
Executive Producer: **ALAN FINE**

Spotlight   **MARVEL**

visit us at www.abdopublishing.com

Reinforced library bound edition published in 2014 by Spotlight, a division of the ABDO Group, PO Box 398166, Minneapolis, Minnesota 55439. Spotlight produces high-quality reinforced library bound editions for schools and libraries. Published by agreement with Marvel Characters, Inc.

Printed in the United States of America, North Mankato, Minnesota.
102013
012014
♻ This book contains at least 10% recycled materials.

MARVEL
Marvel.com
© 2014 Marvel

Library of Congress Cataloging-in-Publication Data

Shanower, Eric.
  The marvelous land of Oz / adapted from the novel by L. Frank Baum ; writer: Eric Shanower ; artist: Skottie Young. -- Reinforced library bound edition.
     pages cm
  "Marvel."
  Summary: When the Scarecrow, now the ruler of the Emerald City, is driven out by General Jinjur and her all-girl army, his friends--the Tin Woodman, a boy named Tip, and Jack Pumpkinhead--try to restore peace in this graphic novel adaptation of L. Frank Baum's classic tale.
  ISBN 978-1-61479-235-2 (vol. 1) -- ISBN 978-1-61479-236-9 (vol. 2) -- ISBN 978-1-61479-237-6 (vol. 3) -- ISBN 978-1-61479-238-3 (vol. 4) -- ISBN 978-1-61479-239-0 (vol. 5) -- ISBN 978-1-61479-240-6 (vol. 6) -- ISBN 978-1-61479-241-3 (vol. 7) -- ISBN 978-1-61479-242-0 (vol. 8)
  1. Graphic novels. [1. Graphic novels. 2. Fantasy.] I. Young, Skottie, illustrator. II. Baum, L. Frank (Lyman Frank), 1856-1919. Marvelous land of Oz. III. Title.
  PZ7.7.S453Mar 2014
  741.5'973--dc23
                    2013030127

All Spotlight books are reinforced library binding and manufactured in the United States of America.

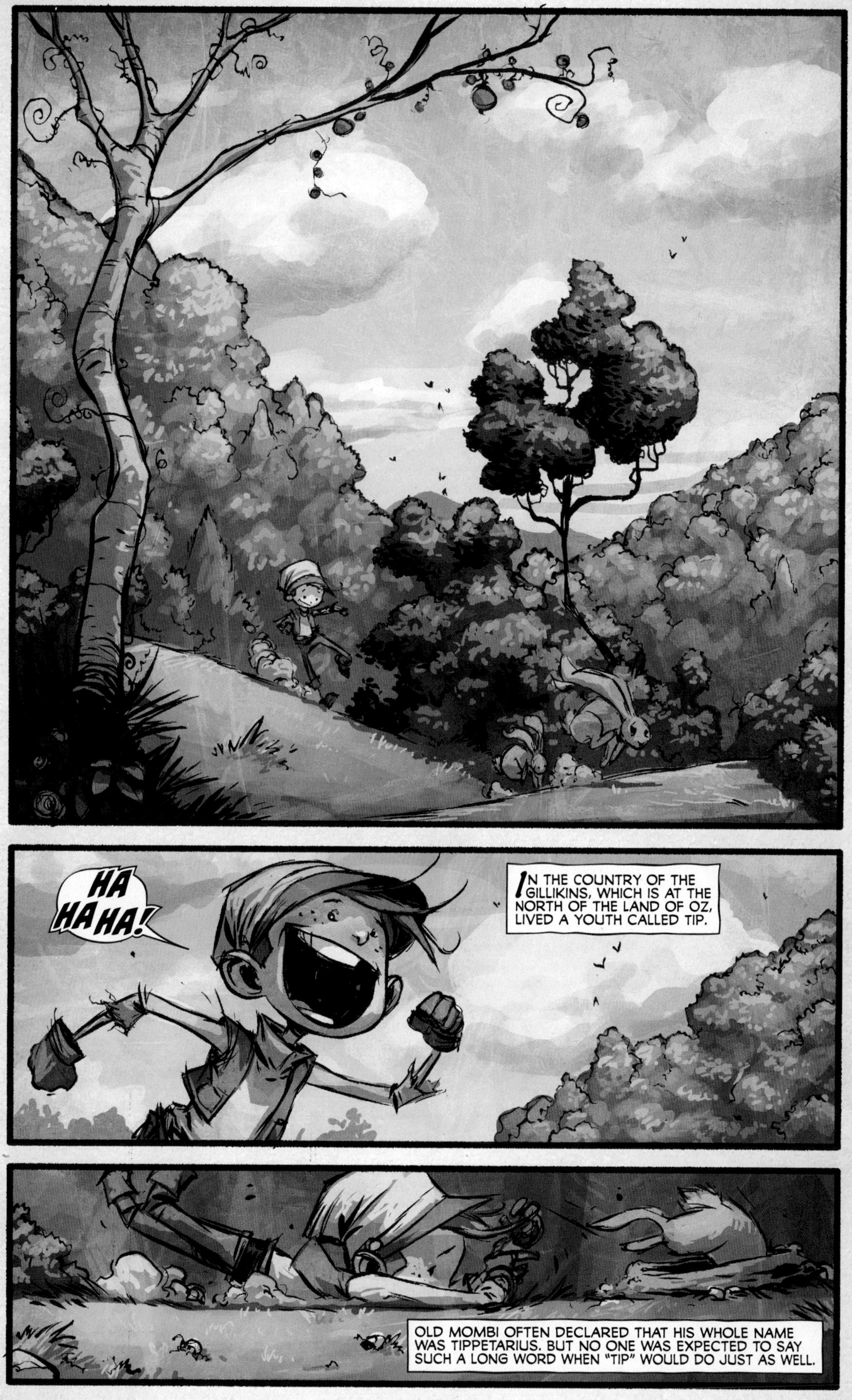
HA HA HA!
IN THE COUNTRY OF THE GILLIKINS, WHICH IS AT THE NORTH OF THE LAND OF OZ, LIVED A YOUTH CALLED TIP.
OLD MOMBI OFTEN DECLARED THAT HIS WHOLE NAME WAS TIPPETARIUS. BUT NO ONE WAS EXPECTED TO SAY SUCH A LONG WORD WHEN "TIP" WOULD DO JUST AS WELL.

THE BOY REMEMBERED NOTHING OF HIS PARENTS, FOR HE HAD BEEN BROUGHT WHEN QUITE YOUNG TO BE REARED BY THE OLD WOMAN KNOWN AS MOMBI.

MOMBI'S REPUTATION WAS NONE OF THE BEST.

THE GILLIKIN PEOPLE HAD REASON TO SUSPECT MOMBI OF INDULGING IN MAGICAL ARTS, AND THEY HESITATED TO ASSOCIATE WITH HER.

HERE'S WOOD TO BOIL YOUR POT.

MOMBI WAS NOT EXACTLY A WITCH. THE GOOD WITCH WHO RULED THAT PART OF THE LAND OF OZ HAD FORBIDDEN ANY OTHER WITCH TO EXIST IN HER DOMINIONS.

WHAT TOOK YOU SO LONG?

SO MOMBI REALIZED IT WAS UNLAWFUL TO BE MORE THAN A SORCERESS, OR AT MOST A WIZARDESS.

BUT MOMBI'S WEIRD POWERS OFTEN FRIGHTENED HER NEIGHBORS.

CLIMBING TREES -- OR CHASING RABBITS --

-- OR FISHING AGAIN!

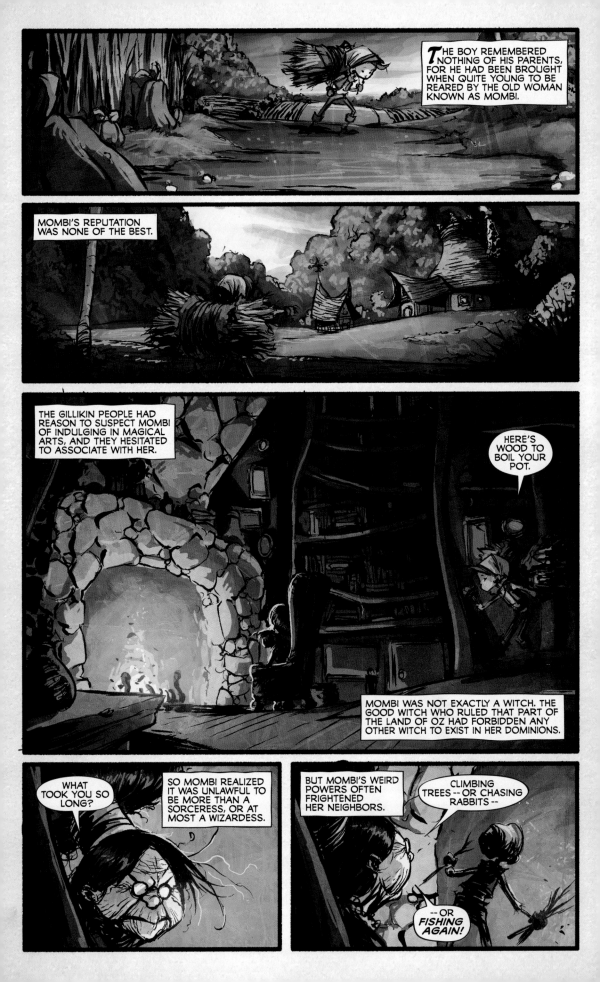

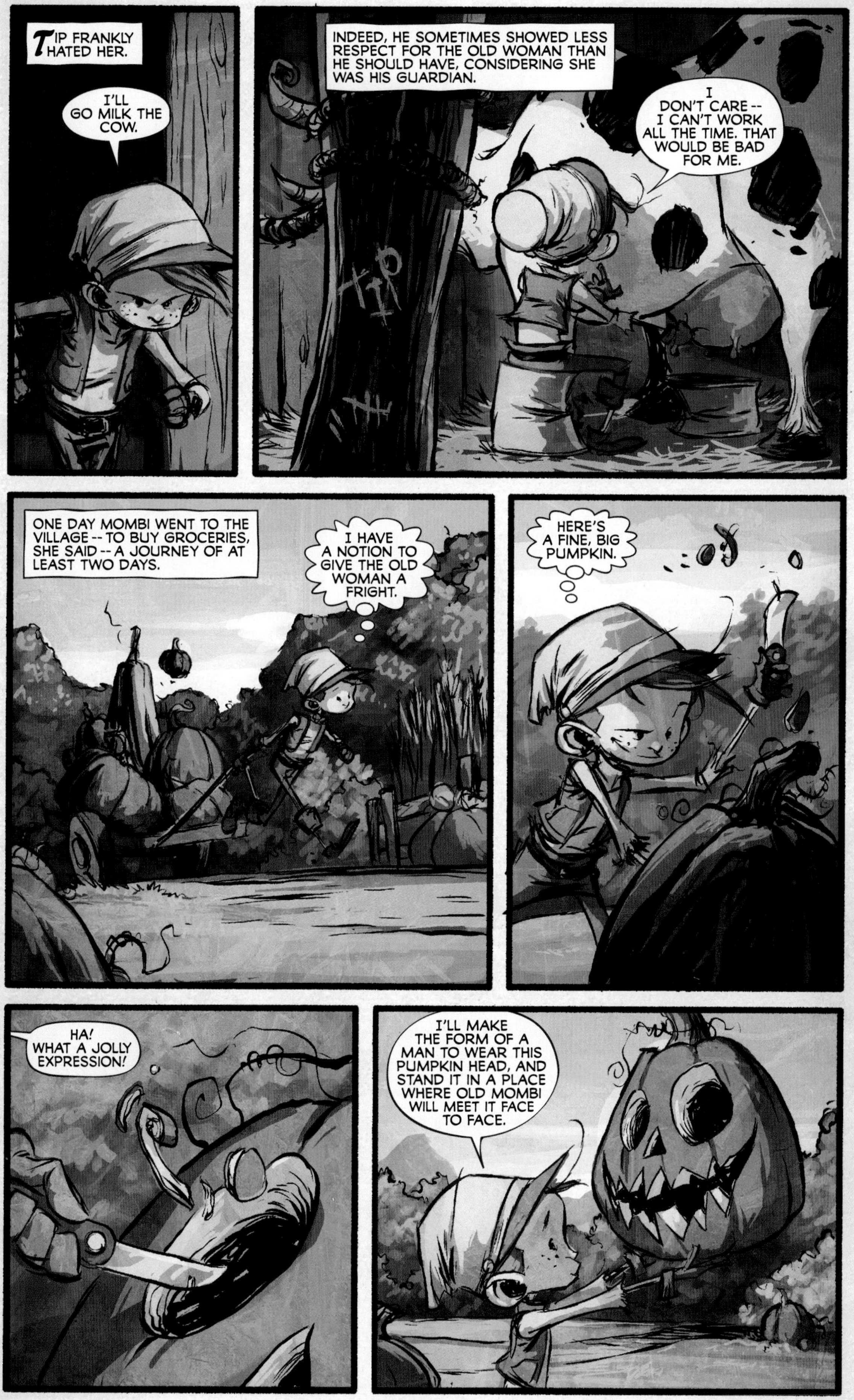
TIP FRANKLY HATED HER.
I'LL GO MILK THE COW.
INDEED, HE SOMETIMES SHOWED LESS RESPECT FOR THE OLD WOMAN THAN HE SHOULD HAVE, CONSIDERING SHE WAS HIS GUARDIAN.
I DON'T CARE -- I CAN'T WORK ALL THE TIME. THAT WOULD BE BAD FOR ME.
TIP
ONE DAY MOMBI WENT TO THE VILLAGE -- TO BUY GROCERIES, SHE SAID -- A JOURNEY OF AT LEAST TWO DAYS.
I HAVE A NOTION TO GIVE THE OLD WOMAN A FRIGHT.
HERE'S A FINE, BIG PUMPKIN.
HA! WHAT A JOLLY EXPRESSION!
I'LL MAKE THE FORM OF A MAN TO WEAR THIS PUMPKIN HEAD, AND STAND IT IN A PLACE WHERE OLD MOMBI WILL MEET IT FACE TO FACE.

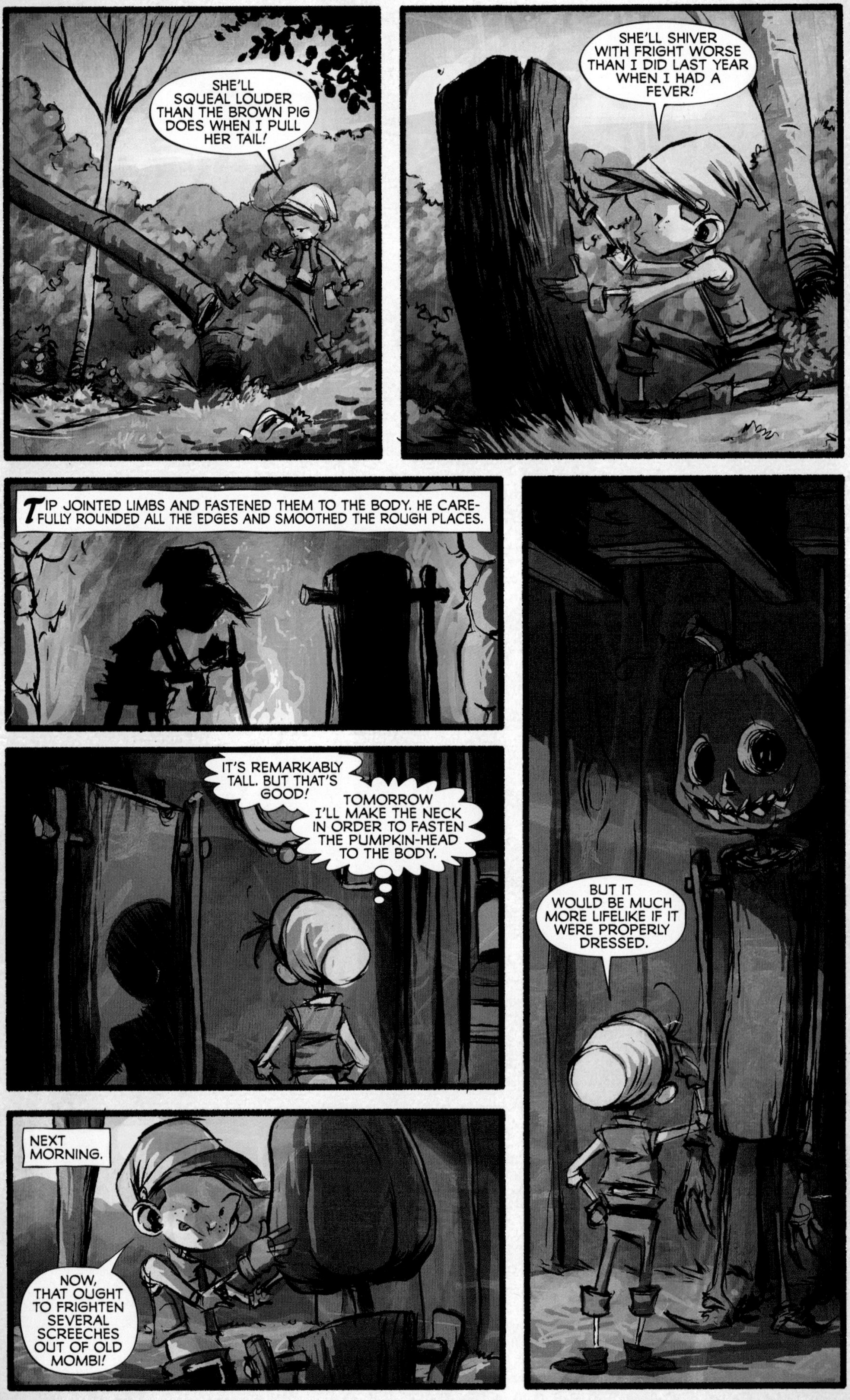
SHE'LL SQUEAL LOUDER THAN THE BROWN PIG DOES WHEN I PULL HER TAIL!
SHE'LL SHIVER WITH FRIGHT WORSE THAN I DID LAST YEAR WHEN I HAD A FEVER!
TIP JOINTED LIMBS AND FASTENED THEM TO THE BODY. HE CAREFULLY ROUNDED ALL THE EDGES AND SMOOTHED THE ROUGH PLACES.
IT'S REMARKABLY TALL. BUT THAT'S GOOD!
TOMORROW I'LL MAKE THE NECK IN ORDER TO FASTEN THE PUMPKIN-HEAD TO THE BODY.
NEXT MORNING.
NOW, THAT OUGHT TO FRIGHTEN SEVERAL SCREECHES OUT OF OLD MOMBI!
BUT IT WOULD BE MUCH MORE LIFELIKE IF IT WERE PROPERLY DRESSED.

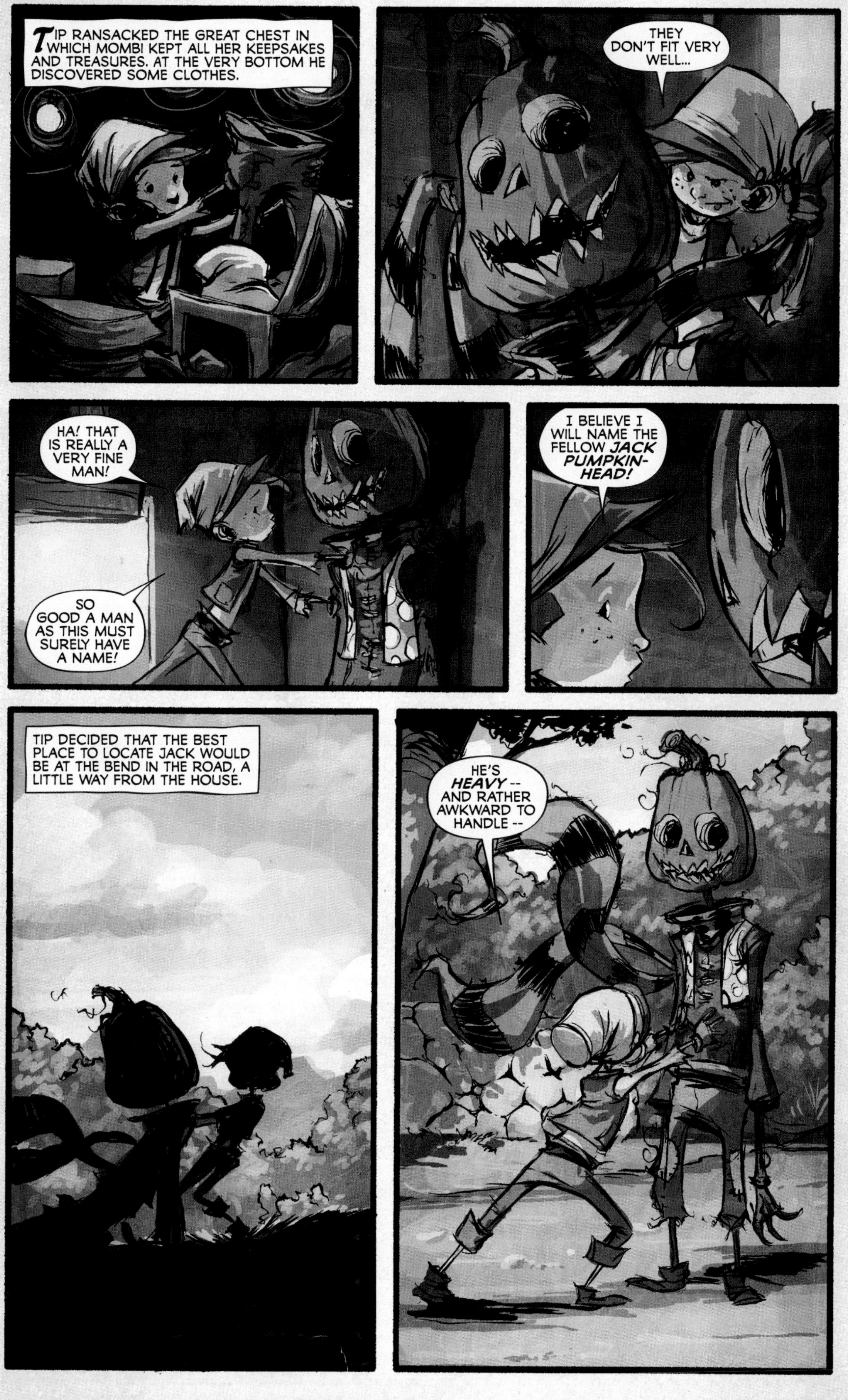
TIP RANSACKED THE GREAT CHEST IN WHICH MOMBI KEPT ALL HER KEEPSAKES AND TREASURES. AT THE VERY BOTTOM HE DISCOVERED SOME CLOTHES.
THEY DON'T FIT VERY WELL...
HA! THAT IS REALLY A VERY FINE MAN!
SO GOOD A MAN AS THIS MUST SURELY HAVE A NAME!
I BELIEVE I WILL NAME THE FELLOW *JACK PUMPKINHEAD!*
TIP DECIDED THAT THE BEST PLACE TO LOCATE JACK WOULD BE AT THE BEND IN THE ROAD, A LITTLE WAY FROM THE HOUSE.
HE'S *HEAVY* -- AND RATHER AWKWARD TO HANDLE --

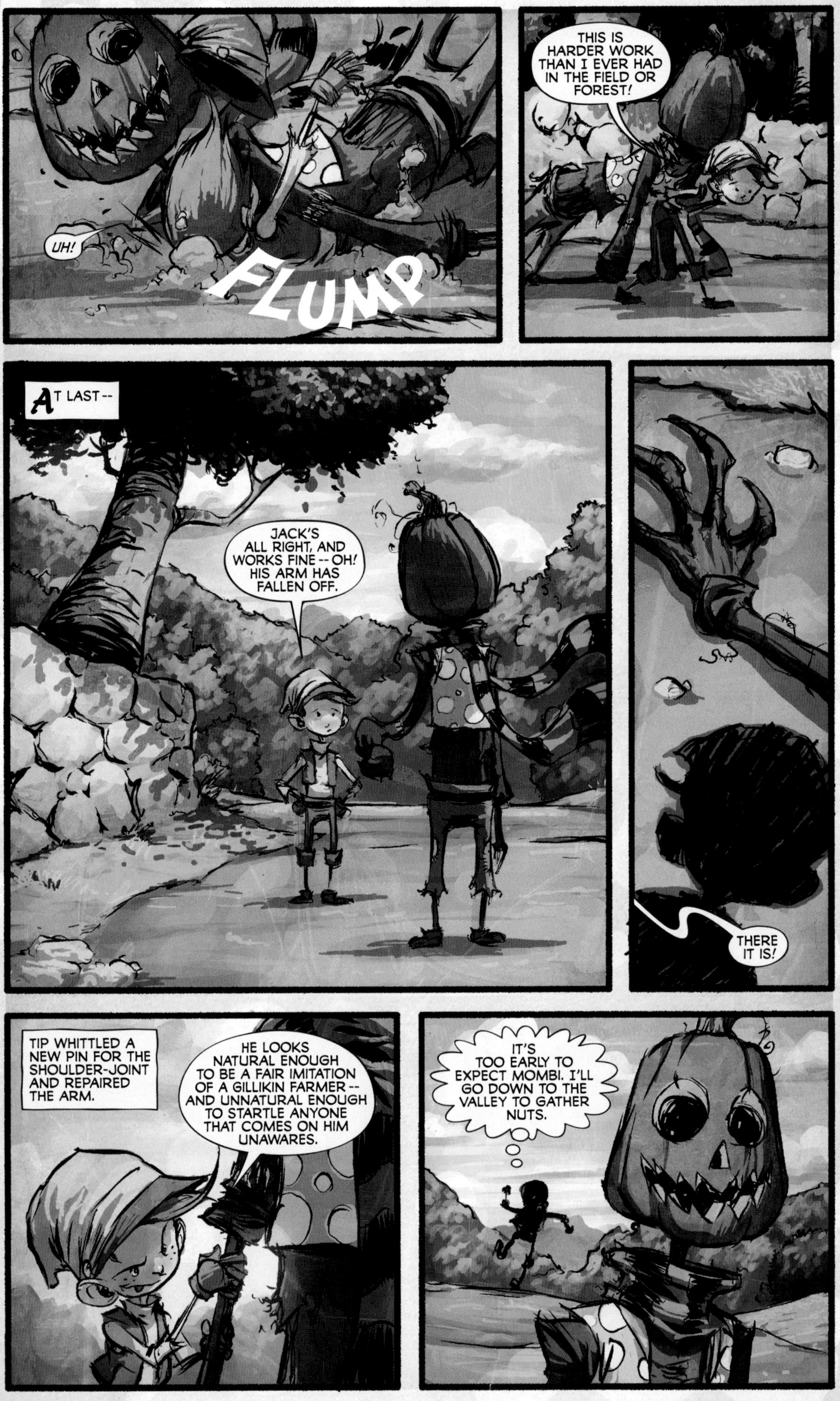
UH!
FLUMP
THIS IS HARDER WORK THAN I EVER HAD IN THE FIELD OR FOREST!
AT LAST--
JACK'S ALL RIGHT, AND WORKS FINE--OH! HIS ARM HAS FALLEN OFF.
THERE IT IS!
TIP WHITTLED A NEW PIN FOR THE SHOULDER-JOINT AND REPAIRED THE ARM.
HE LOOKS NATURAL ENOUGH TO BE A FAIR IMITATION OF A GILLIKIN FARMER-- AND UNNATURAL ENOUGH TO STARTLE ANYONE THAT COMES ON HIM UNAWARES.
IT'S TOO EARLY TO EXPECT MOMBI. I'LL GO DOWN TO THE VALLEY TO GATHER NUTS.

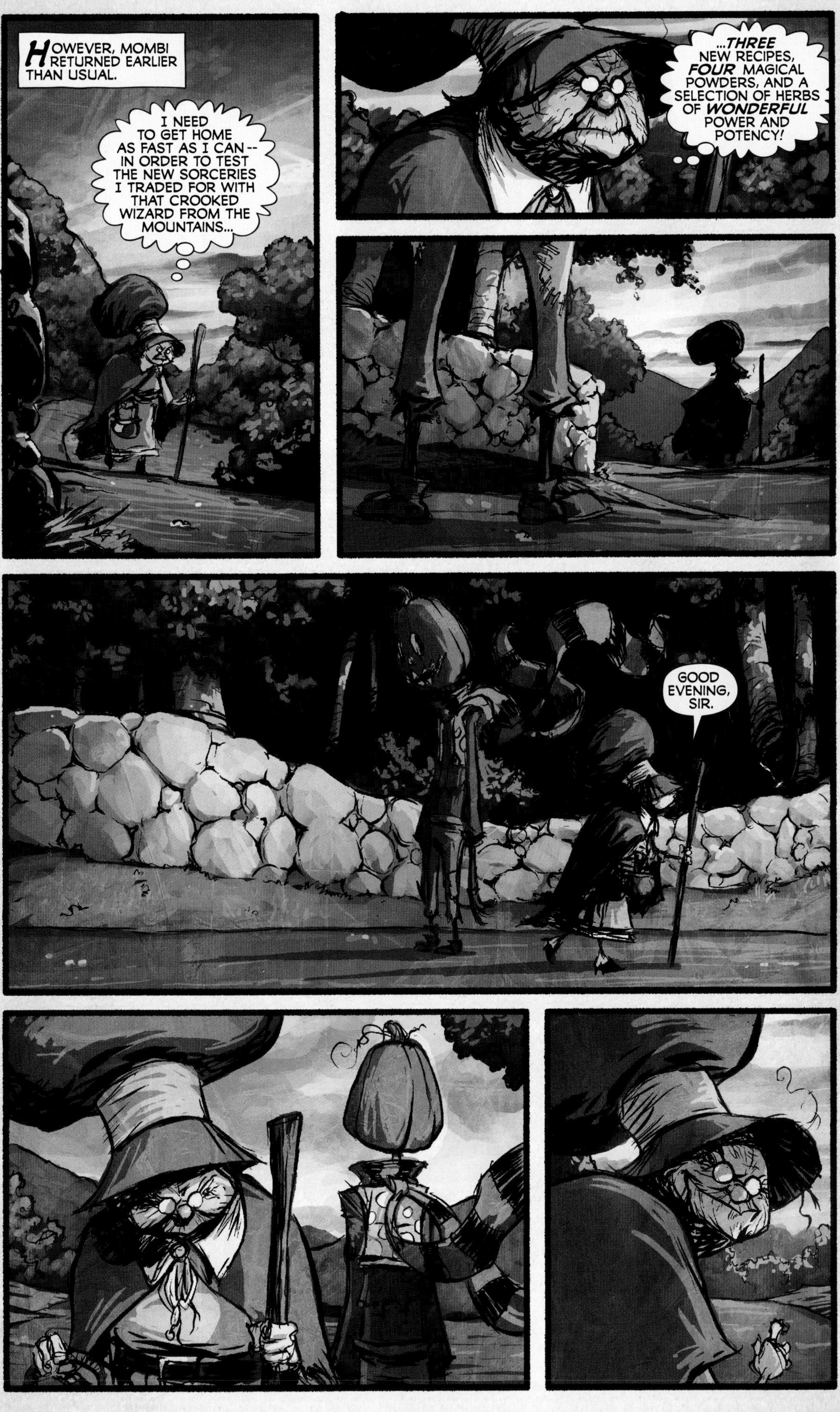
HOWEVER, MOMBI RETURNED EARLIER THAN USUAL.
I NEED TO GET HOME AS FAST AS I CAN -- IN ORDER TO TEST THE NEW SORCERIES I TRADED FOR WITH THAT CROOKED WIZARD FROM THE MOUNTAINS...
...THREE NEW RECIPES, FOUR MAGICAL POWDERS, AND A SELECTION OF HERBS OF WONDERFUL POWER AND POTENCY!
GOOD EVENING, SIR.

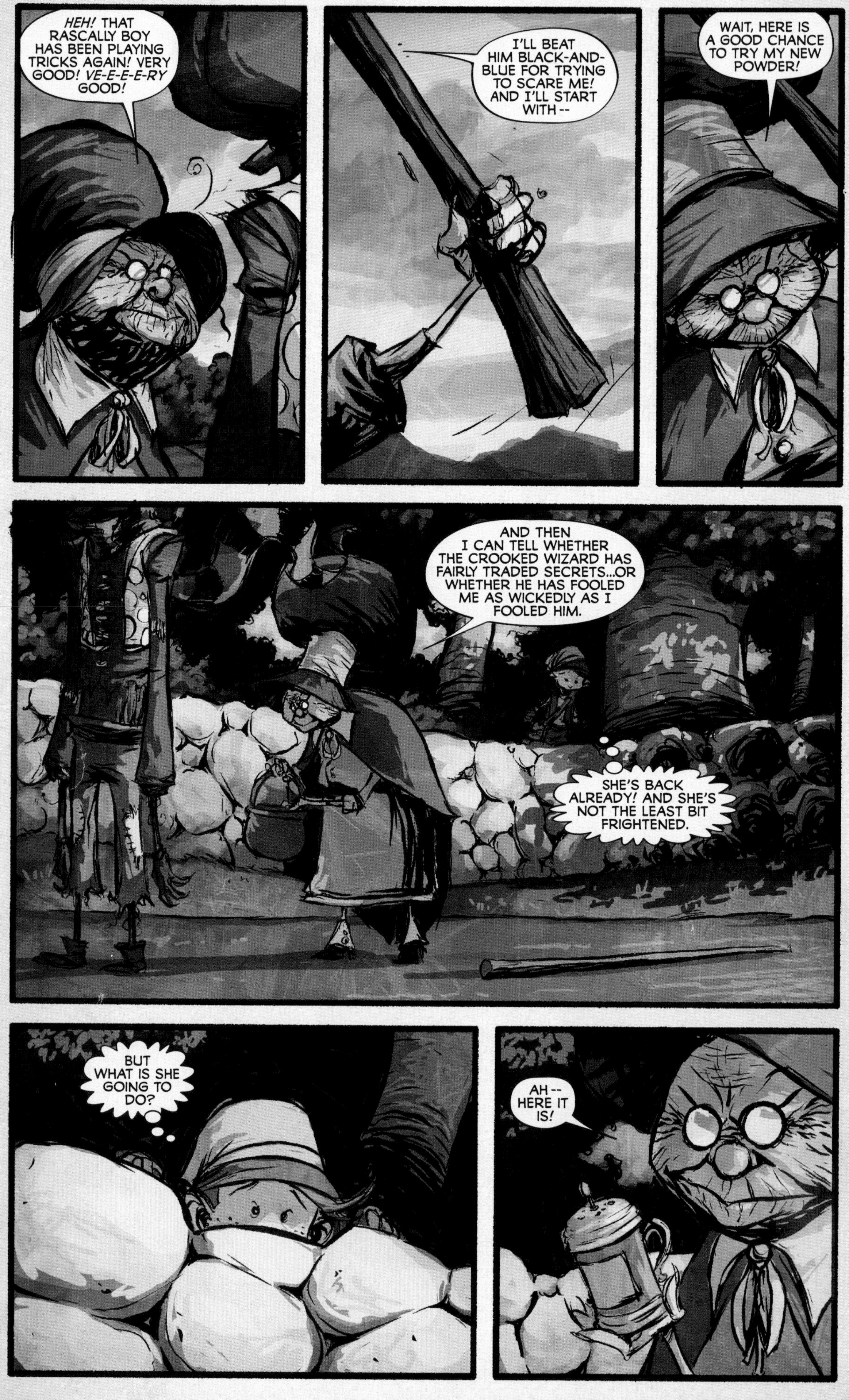

HEH! THAT RASCALLY BOY HAS BEEN PLAYING TRICKS AGAIN! VERY GOOD! *VE-E-E-E-RY* GOOD!
I'LL BEAT HIM BLACK-AND-BLUE FOR TRYING TO SCARE ME! AND I'LL START WITH --
WAIT, HERE IS A GOOD CHANCE TO TRY MY NEW POWDER!
AND THEN I CAN TELL WHETHER THE CROOKED WIZARD HAS FAIRLY TRADED SECRETS...OR WHETHER HE HAS FOOLED ME AS WICKEDLY AS I FOOLED HIM.
SHE'S BACK ALREADY! AND SHE'S NOT THE LEAST BIT FRIGHTENED.
BUT WHAT IS SHE GOING TO DO?
AH -- HERE IT IS!

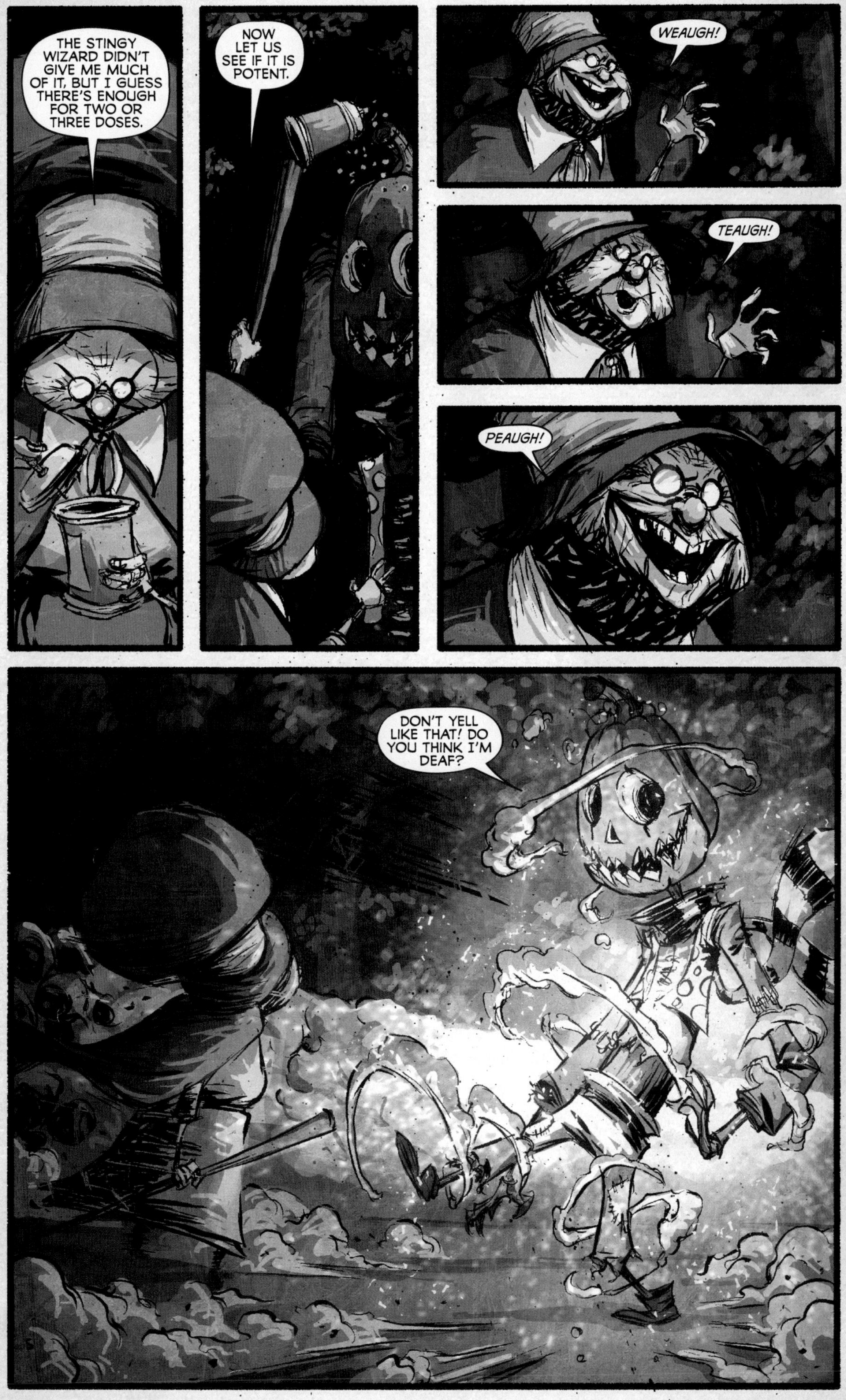
THE STINGY WIZARD DIDN'T GIVE ME MUCH OF IT, BUT I GUESS THERE'S ENOUGH FOR TWO OR THREE DOSES.
NOW LET US SEE IF IT IS POTENT.
WEAUGH!
TEAUGH!
PEAUGH!
DON'T YELL LIKE THAT! DO YOU THINK I'M DEAF?

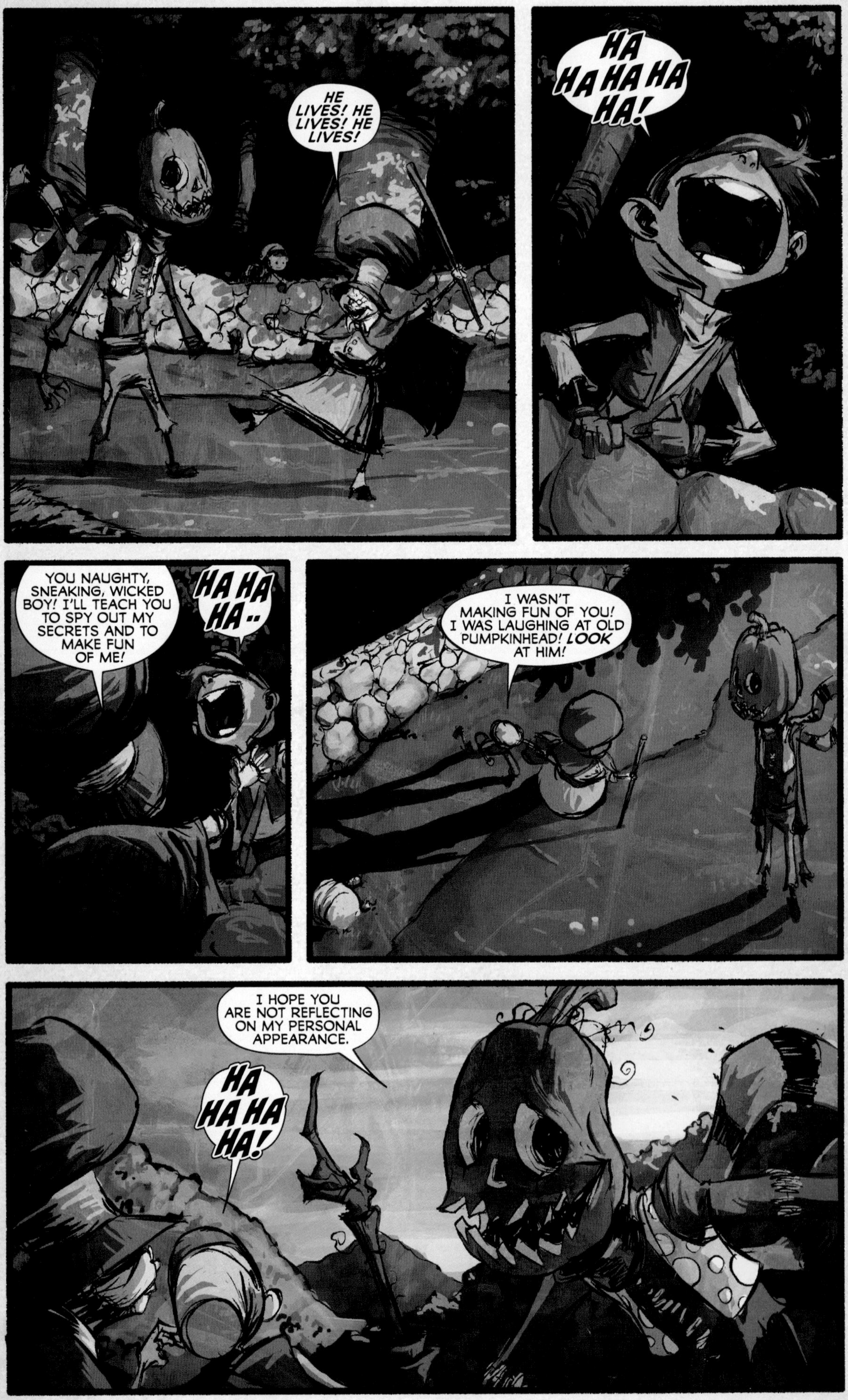
HE LIVES! HE LIVES! HE LIVES!
HA HA HA HA HA HA!
YOU NAUGHTY, SNEAKING, WICKED BOY! I'LL TEACH YOU TO SPY OUT MY SECRETS AND TO MAKE FUN OF ME!
HA HA HA..
I WASN'T MAKING FUN OF YOU! I WAS LAUGHING AT OLD PUMPKINHEAD! LOOK AT HIM!
I HOPE YOU ARE NOT REFLECTING ON MY PERSONAL APPEARANCE.
HA HA HA HA HA!

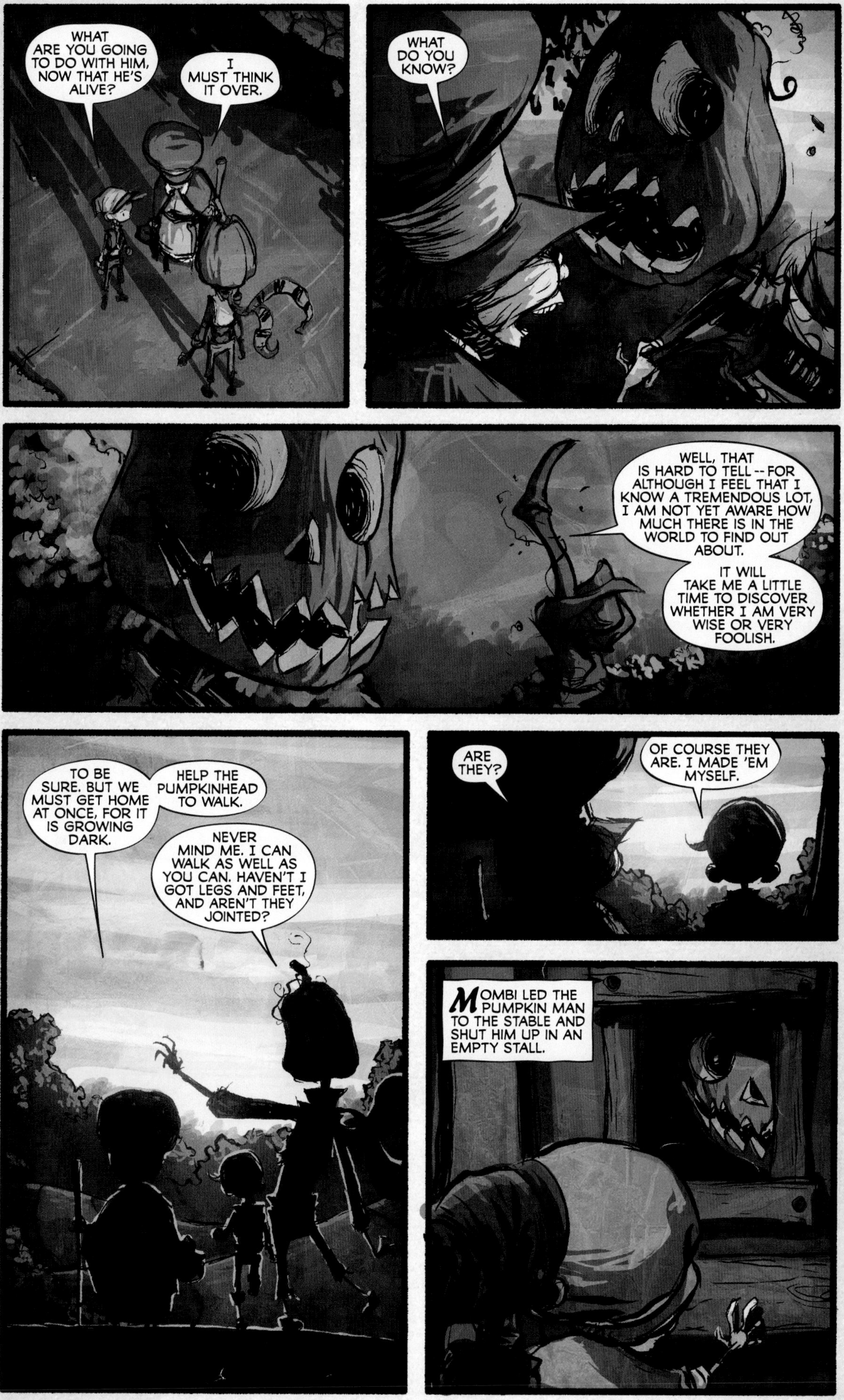
WHAT ARE YOU GOING TO DO WITH HIM, NOW THAT HE'S ALIVE?
I MUST THINK IT OVER.
WHAT DO YOU KNOW?
WELL, THAT IS HARD TO TELL -- FOR ALTHOUGH I FEEL THAT I KNOW A TREMENDOUS LOT, I AM NOT YET AWARE HOW MUCH THERE IS IN THE WORLD TO FIND OUT ABOUT.
IT WILL TAKE ME A LITTLE TIME TO DISCOVER WHETHER I AM VERY WISE OR VERY FOOLISH.
HELP THE PUMPKINHEAD TO WALK.
TO BE SURE. BUT WE MUST GET HOME AT ONCE, FOR IT IS GROWING DARK.
NEVER MIND ME. I CAN WALK AS WELL AS YOU CAN. HAVEN'T I GOT LEGS AND FEET, AND AREN'T THEY JOINTED?
ARE THEY?
OF COURSE THEY ARE. I MADE 'EM MYSELF.
MOMBI LED THE PUMPKIN MAN TO THE STABLE AND SHUT HIM UP IN AN EMPTY STALL.

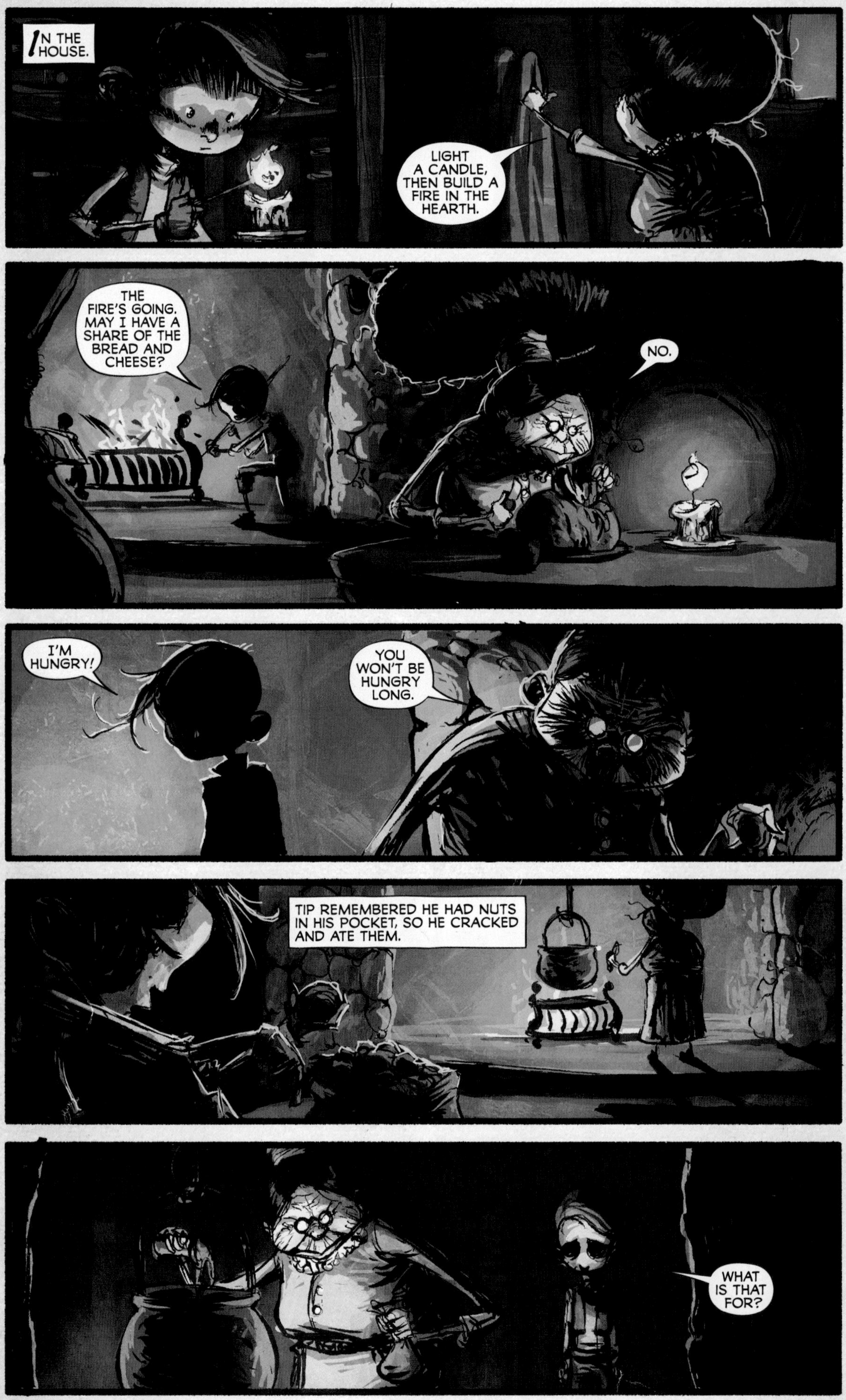
IN THE HOUSE.
LIGHT A CANDLE, THEN BUILD A FIRE IN THE HEARTH.
THE FIRE'S GOING. MAY I HAVE A SHARE OF THE BREAD AND CHEESE?
NO.
I'M HUNGRY!
YOU WON'T BE HUNGRY LONG.
TIP REMEMBERED HE HAD NUTS IN HIS POCKET, SO HE CRACKED AND ATE THEM.
WHAT IS THAT FOR?

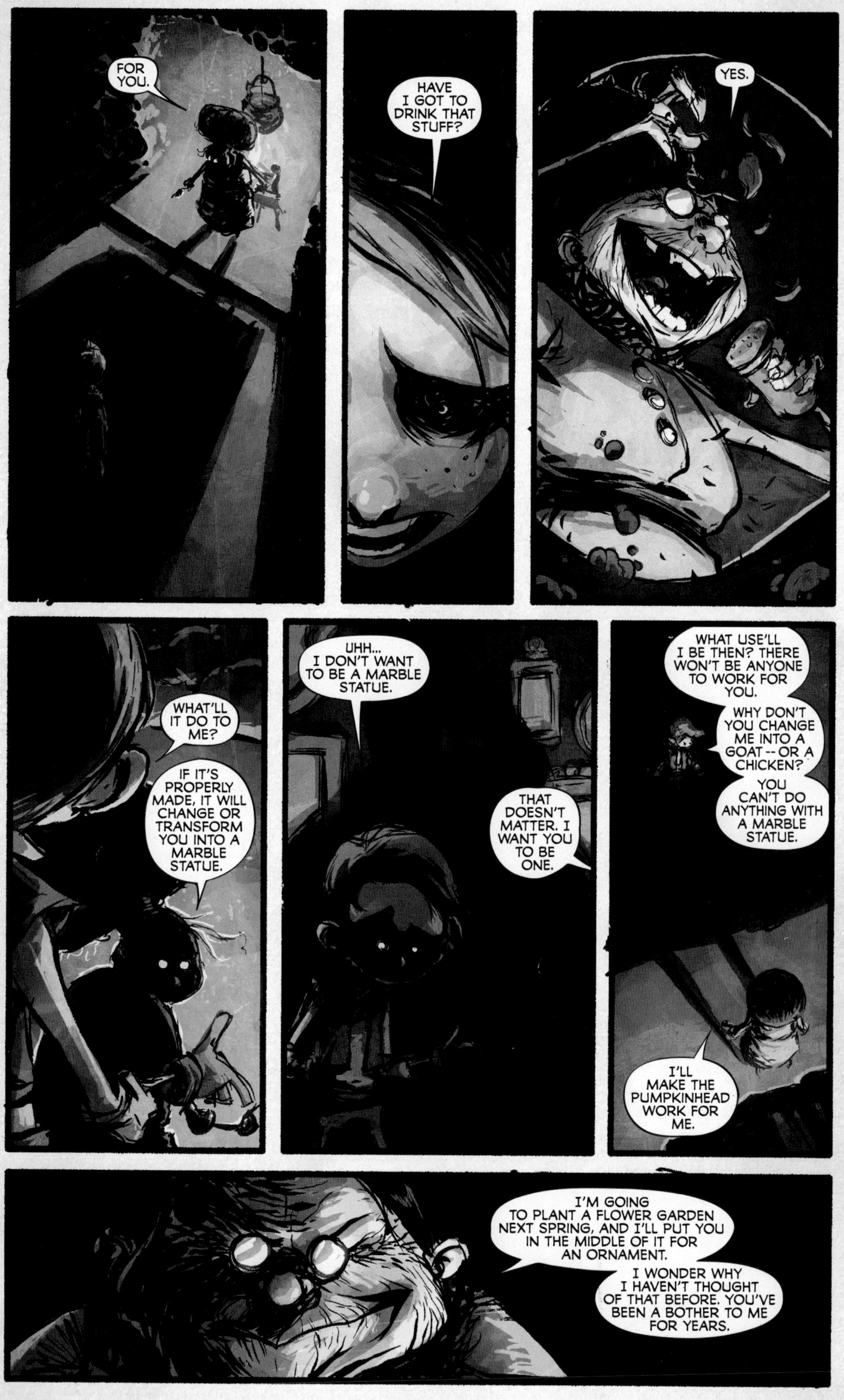
FOR YOU.
HAVE I GOT TO DRINK THAT STUFF?
YES.
WHAT'LL IT DO TO ME?
IF IT'S PROPERLY MADE, IT WILL CHANGE OR TRANSFORM YOU INTO A MARBLE STATUE.
UHH... I DON'T WANT TO BE A MARBLE STATUE.
THAT DOESN'T MATTER. I WANT YOU TO BE ONE.
WHAT USE'LL I BE THEN? THERE WON'T BE ANYONE TO WORK FOR YOU.
WHY DON'T YOU CHANGE ME INTO A GOAT -- OR A CHICKEN?
YOU CAN'T DO ANYTHING WITH A MARBLE STATUE.
I'LL MAKE THE PUMPKINHEAD WORK FOR ME.
I'M GOING TO PLANT A FLOWER GARDEN NEXT SPRING, AND I'LL PUT YOU IN THE MIDDLE OF IT FOR AN ORNAMENT.
I WONDER WHY I HAVEN'T THOUGHT OF THAT BEFORE. YOU'VE BEEN A BOTHER TO ME FOR YEARS.

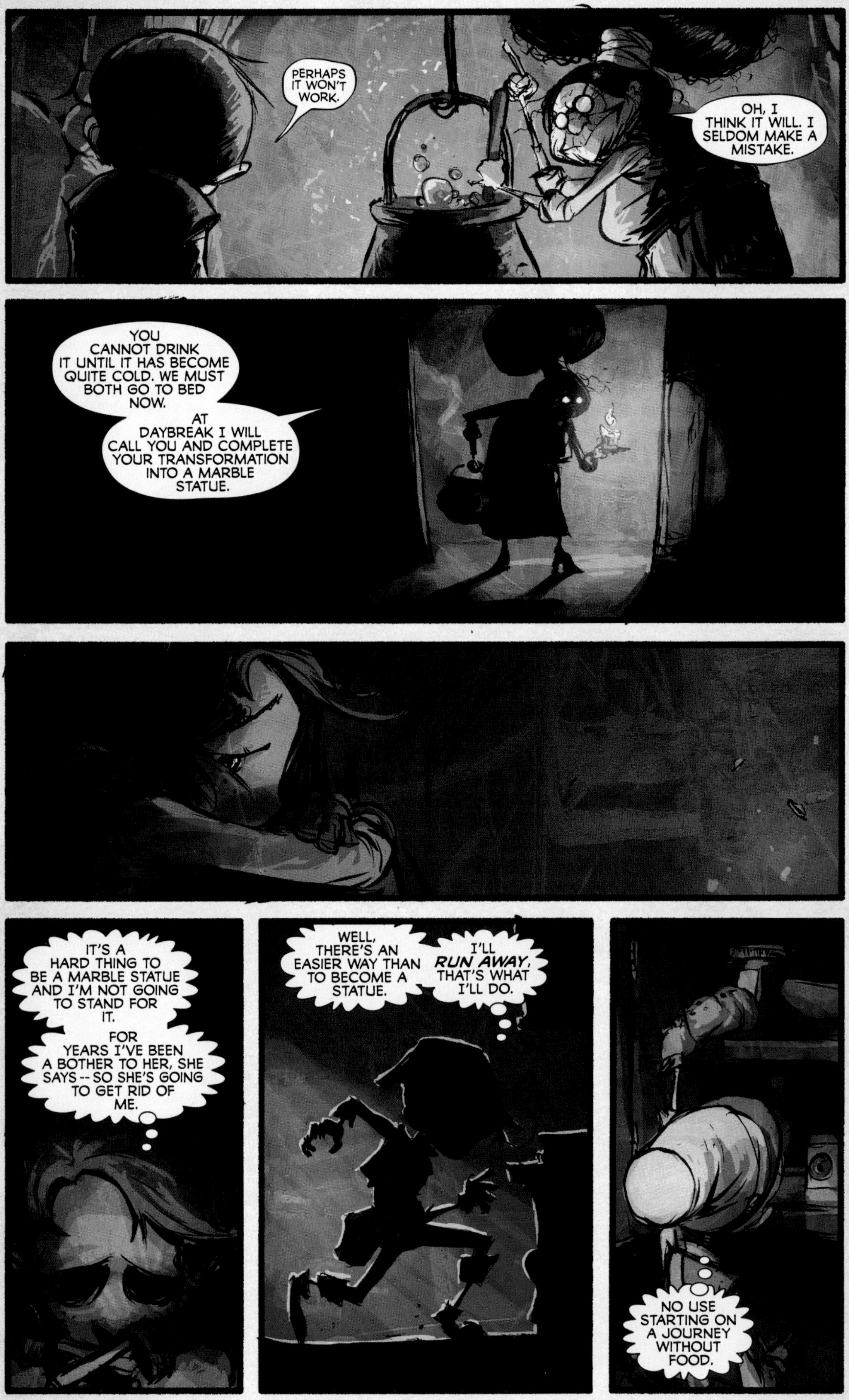
PERHAPS IT WON'T WORK.
OH, I THINK IT WILL. I SELDOM MAKE A MISTAKE.
YOU CANNOT DRINK IT UNTIL IT HAS BECOME QUITE COLD. WE MUST BOTH GO TO BED NOW.
AT DAYBREAK I WILL CALL YOU AND COMPLETE YOUR TRANSFORMATION INTO A MARBLE STATUE.
IT'S A HARD THING TO BE A MARBLE STATUE AND I'M NOT GOING TO STAND FOR IT.
FOR YEARS I'VE BEEN A BOTHER TO HER, SHE SAYS -- SO SHE'S GOING TO GET RID OF ME.
WELL, THERE'S AN EASIER WAY THAN TO BECOME A STATUE.
I'LL *RUN AWAY*, THAT'S WHAT I'LL DO.
NO USE STARTING ON A JOURNEY WITHOUT FOOD.

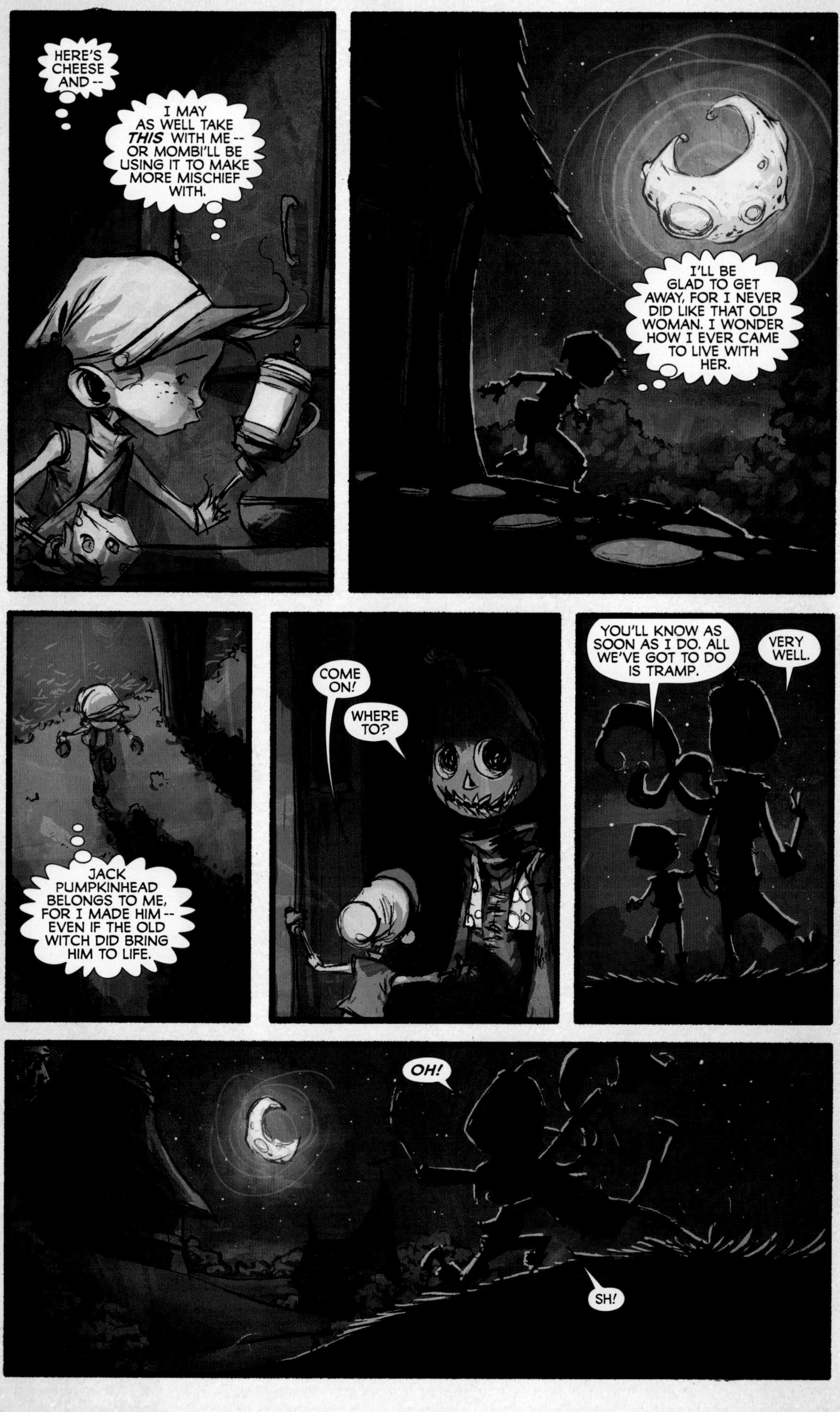
HERE'S CHEESE AND --
I MAY AS WELL TAKE *THIS* WITH ME -- OR MOMBI'LL BE USING IT TO MAKE MORE MISCHIEF WITH.
I'LL BE GLAD TO GET AWAY, FOR I NEVER DID LIKE THAT OLD WOMAN. I WONDER HOW I EVER CAME TO LIVE WITH HER.
JACK PUMPKINHEAD BELONGS TO ME, FOR I MADE HIM -- EVEN IF THE OLD WITCH DID BRING HIM TO LIFE.
COME ON!
WHERE TO?
YOU'LL KNOW AS SOON AS I DO. ALL WE'VE GOT TO DO IS TRAMP.
VERY WELL.
OH!
SH!

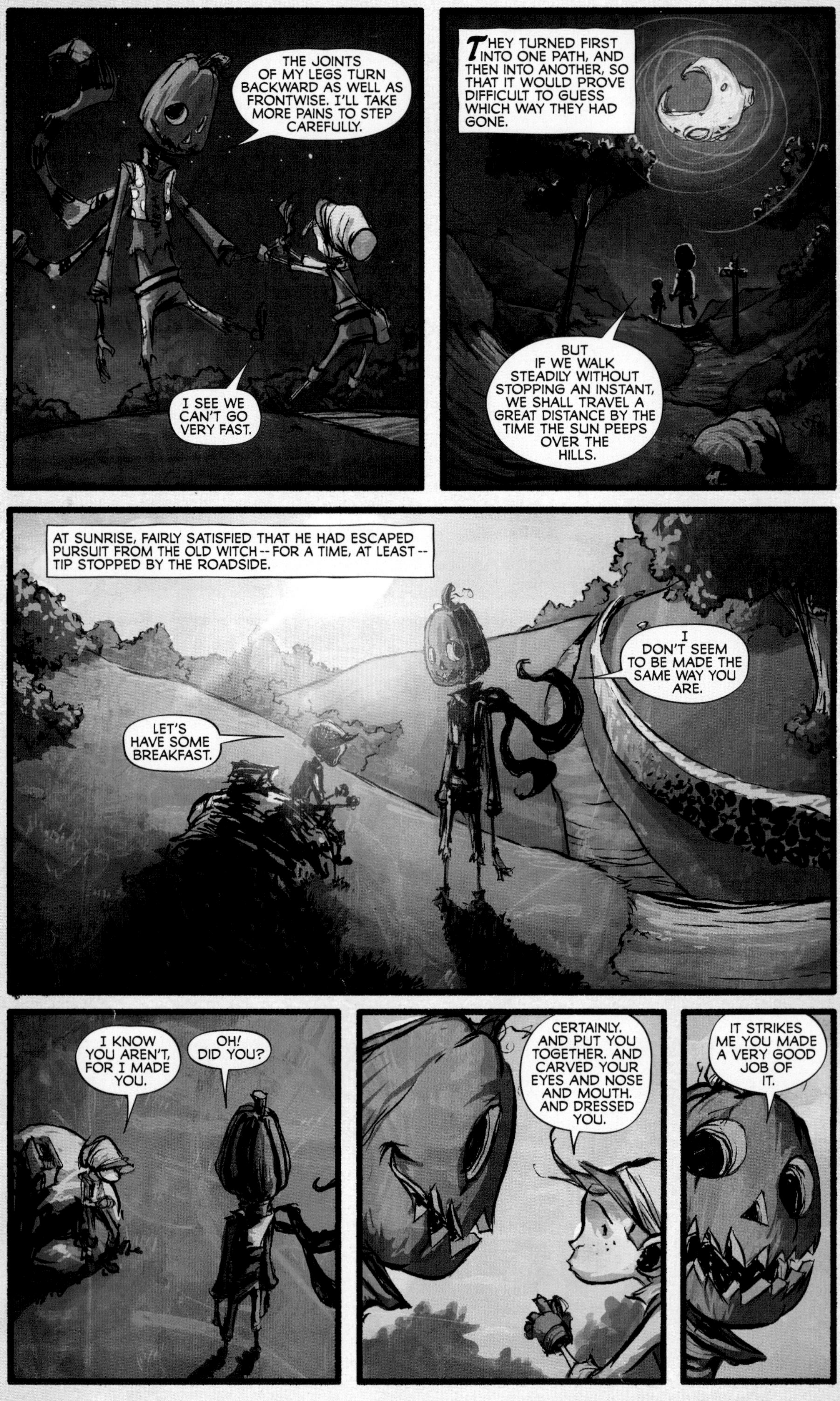
THE JOINTS OF MY LEGS TURN BACKWARD AS WELL AS FRONTWISE. I'LL TAKE MORE PAINS TO STEP CAREFULLY.
I SEE WE CAN'T GO VERY FAST.
THEY TURNED FIRST INTO ONE PATH, AND THEN INTO ANOTHER, SO THAT IT WOULD PROVE DIFFICULT TO GUESS WHICH WAY THEY HAD GONE.
BUT IF WE WALK STEADILY WITHOUT STOPPING AN INSTANT, WE SHALL TRAVEL A GREAT DISTANCE BY THE TIME THE SUN PEEPS OVER THE HILLS.
AT SUNRISE, FAIRLY SATISFIED THAT HE HAD ESCAPED PURSUIT FROM THE OLD WITCH -- FOR A TIME, AT LEAST -- TIP STOPPED BY THE ROADSIDE.
LET'S HAVE SOME BREAKFAST.
I DON'T SEEM TO BE MADE THE SAME WAY YOU ARE.
I KNOW YOU AREN'T, FOR I MADE YOU.
OH! DID YOU?
CERTAINLY. AND PUT YOU TOGETHER. AND CARVED YOUR EYES AND NOSE AND MOUTH. AND DRESSED YOU.
IT STRIKES ME YOU MADE A VERY GOOD JOB OF IT.

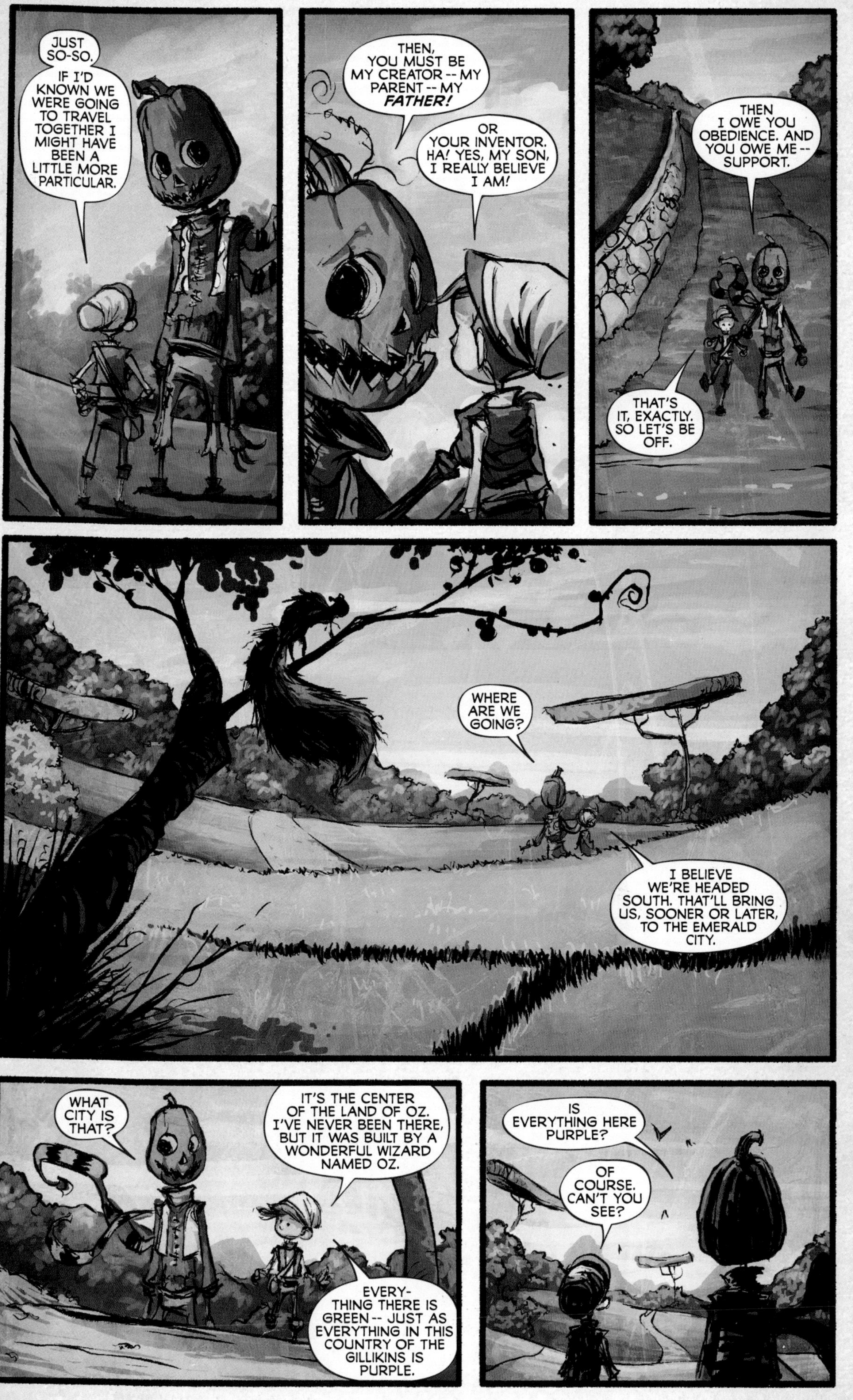
JUST SO-SO.
IF I'D KNOWN WE WERE GOING TO TRAVEL TOGETHER I MIGHT HAVE BEEN A LITTLE MORE PARTICULAR.
THEN, YOU MUST BE MY CREATOR -- MY PARENT -- MY FATHER!
OR YOUR INVENTOR. HA! YES, MY SON, I REALLY BELIEVE I AM!
THEN I OWE YOU OBEDIENCE. AND YOU OWE ME -- SUPPORT.
THAT'S IT, EXACTLY. SO LET'S BE OFF.
WHERE ARE WE GOING?
I BELIEVE WE'RE HEADED SOUTH. THAT'LL BRING US, SOONER OR LATER, TO THE EMERALD CITY.
WHAT CITY IS THAT?
IT'S THE CENTER OF THE LAND OF OZ. I'VE NEVER BEEN THERE, BUT IT WAS BUILT BY A WONDERFUL WIZARD NAMED OZ.
EVERY-THING THERE IS GREEN -- JUST AS EVERYTHING IN THIS COUNTRY OF THE GILLIKINS IS PURPLE.
IS EVERYTHING HERE PURPLE?
OF COURSE. CAN'T YOU SEE?

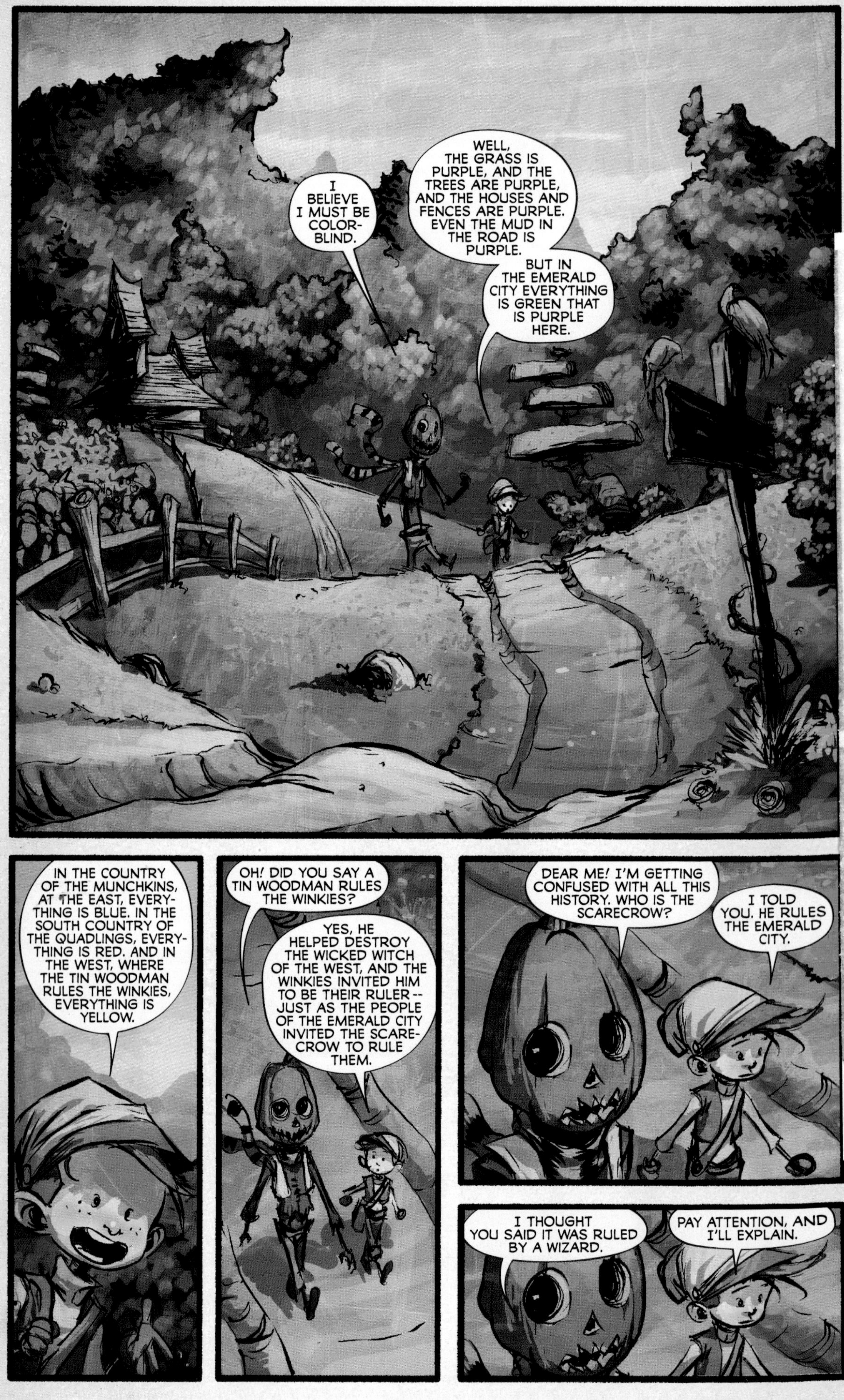
I BELIEVE I MUST BE COLOR-BLIND.
WELL, THE GRASS IS PURPLE, AND THE TREES ARE PURPLE, AND THE HOUSES AND FENCES ARE PURPLE. EVEN THE MUD IN THE ROAD IS PURPLE.
BUT IN THE EMERALD CITY EVERYTHING IS GREEN THAT IS PURPLE HERE.
IN THE COUNTRY OF THE MUNCHKINS, AT THE EAST, EVERY-THING IS BLUE. IN THE SOUTH COUNTRY OF THE QUADLINGS, EVERY-THING IS RED. AND IN THE WEST, WHERE THE TIN WOODMAN RULES THE WINKIES, EVERYTHING IS YELLOW.
OH! DID YOU SAY A TIN WOODMAN RULES THE WINKIES?
YES, HE HELPED DESTROY THE WICKED WITCH OF THE WEST, AND THE WINKIES INVITED HIM TO BE THEIR RULER -- JUST AS THE PEOPLE OF THE EMERALD CITY INVITED THE SCARE-CROW TO RULE THEM.
DEAR ME! I'M GETTING CONFUSED WITH ALL THIS HISTORY. WHO IS THE SCARECROW?
I TOLD YOU. HE RULES THE EMERALD CITY.
I THOUGHT YOU SAID IT WAS RULED BY A WIZARD.
PAY ATTENTION, AND I'LL EXPLAIN.

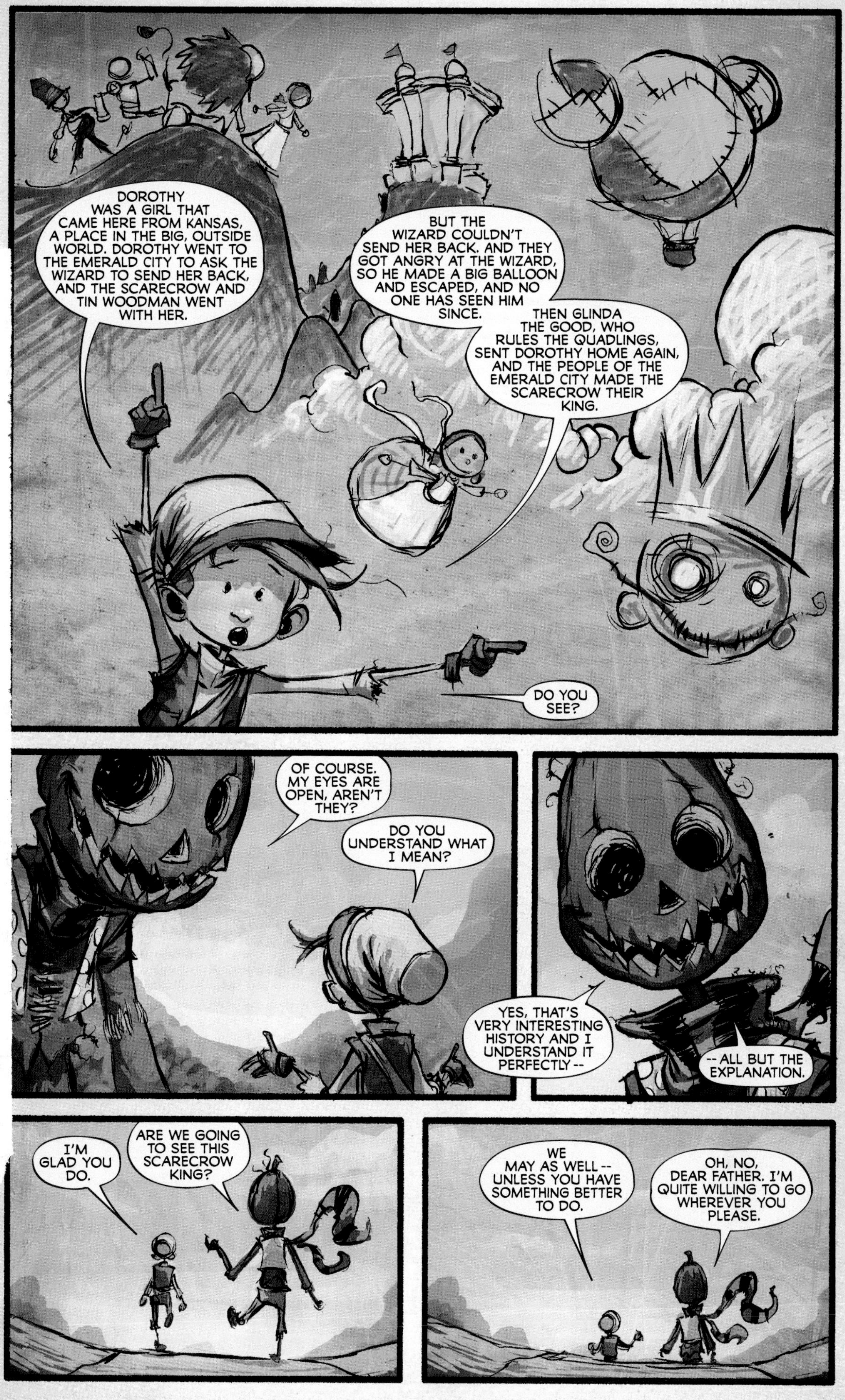
DOROTHY WAS A GIRL THAT CAME HERE FROM KANSAS, A PLACE IN THE BIG, OUTSIDE WORLD. DOROTHY WENT TO THE EMERALD CITY TO ASK THE WIZARD TO SEND HER BACK, AND THE SCARECROW AND TIN WOODMAN WENT WITH HER.
BUT THE WIZARD COULDN'T SEND HER BACK. AND THEY GOT ANGRY AT THE WIZARD, SO HE MADE A BIG BALLOON AND ESCAPED, AND NO ONE HAS SEEN HIM SINCE.
THEN GLINDA THE GOOD, WHO RULES THE QUADLINGS, SENT DOROTHY HOME AGAIN, AND THE PEOPLE OF THE EMERALD CITY MADE THE SCARECROW THEIR KING.
DO YOU SEE?
OF COURSE. MY EYES ARE OPEN, AREN'T THEY?
DO YOU UNDERSTAND WHAT I MEAN?
YES, THAT'S VERY INTERESTING HISTORY AND I UNDERSTAND IT PERFECTLY --
-- ALL BUT THE EXPLANATION.
I'M GLAD YOU DO.
ARE WE GOING TO SEE THIS SCARECROW KING?
WE MAY AS WELL -- UNLESS YOU HAVE SOMETHING BETTER TO DO.
OH, NO, DEAR FATHER. I'M QUITE WILLING TO GO WHEREVER YOU PLEASE.

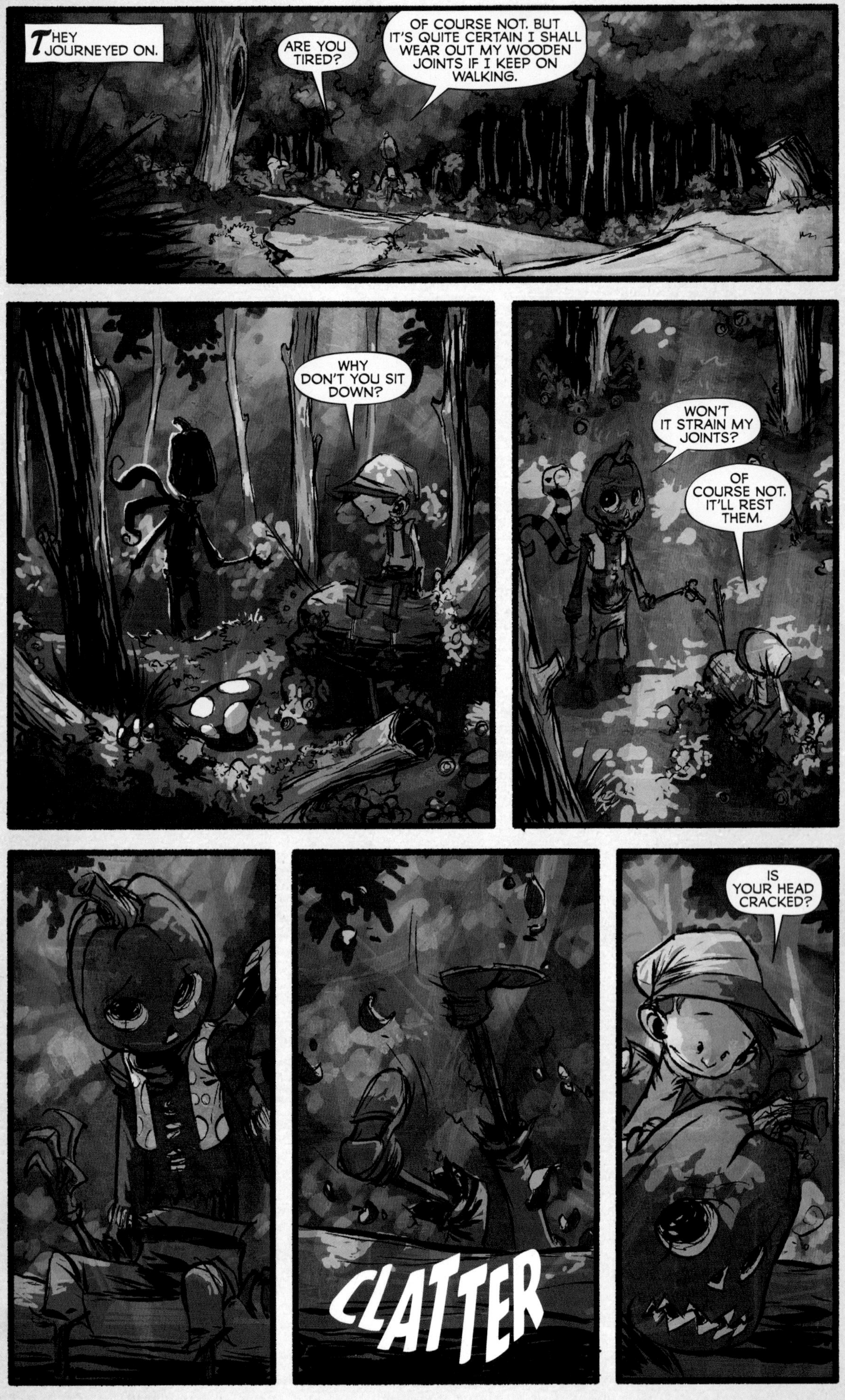
THEY JOURNEYED ON.
ARE YOU TIRED?
OF COURSE NOT. BUT IT'S QUITE CERTAIN I SHALL WEAR OUT MY WOODEN JOINTS IF I KEEP ON WALKING.
WHY DON'T YOU SIT DOWN?
WON'T IT STRAIN MY JOINTS?
OF COURSE NOT. IT'LL REST THEM.
CLATTER
IS YOUR HEAD CRACKED?

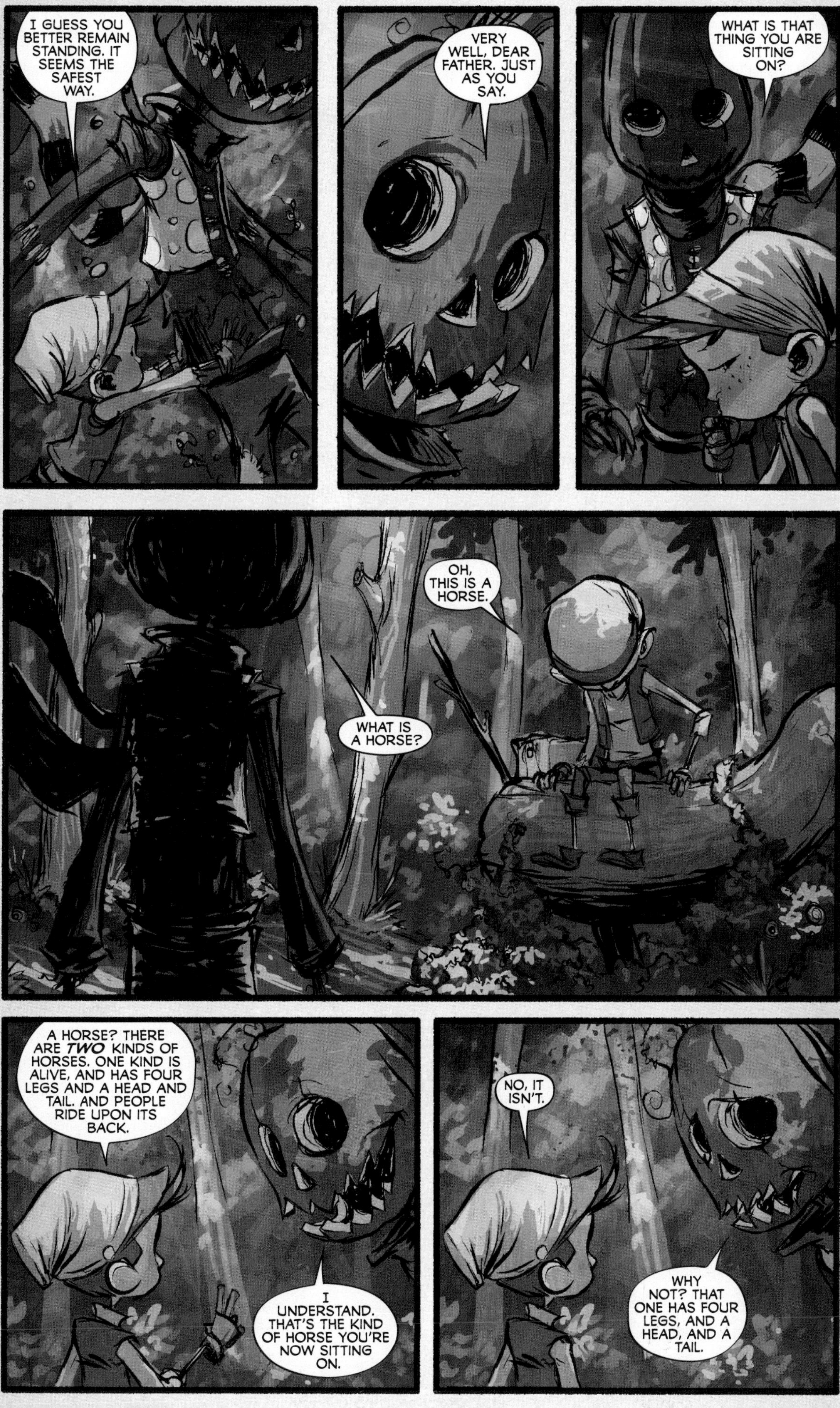
I GUESS YOU BETTER REMAIN STANDING. IT SEEMS THE SAFEST WAY.
VERY WELL, DEAR FATHER. JUST AS YOU SAY.
WHAT IS THAT THING YOU ARE SITTING ON?
OH, THIS IS A HORSE.
WHAT IS A HORSE?
A HORSE? THERE ARE *TWO* KINDS OF HORSES. ONE KIND IS ALIVE, AND HAS FOUR LEGS AND A HEAD AND TAIL. AND PEOPLE RIDE UPON ITS BACK.
I UNDERSTAND. THAT'S THE KIND OF HORSE YOU'RE NOW SITTING ON.
NO, IT ISN'T.
WHY NOT? THAT ONE HAS FOUR LEGS, AND A HEAD, AND A TAIL.

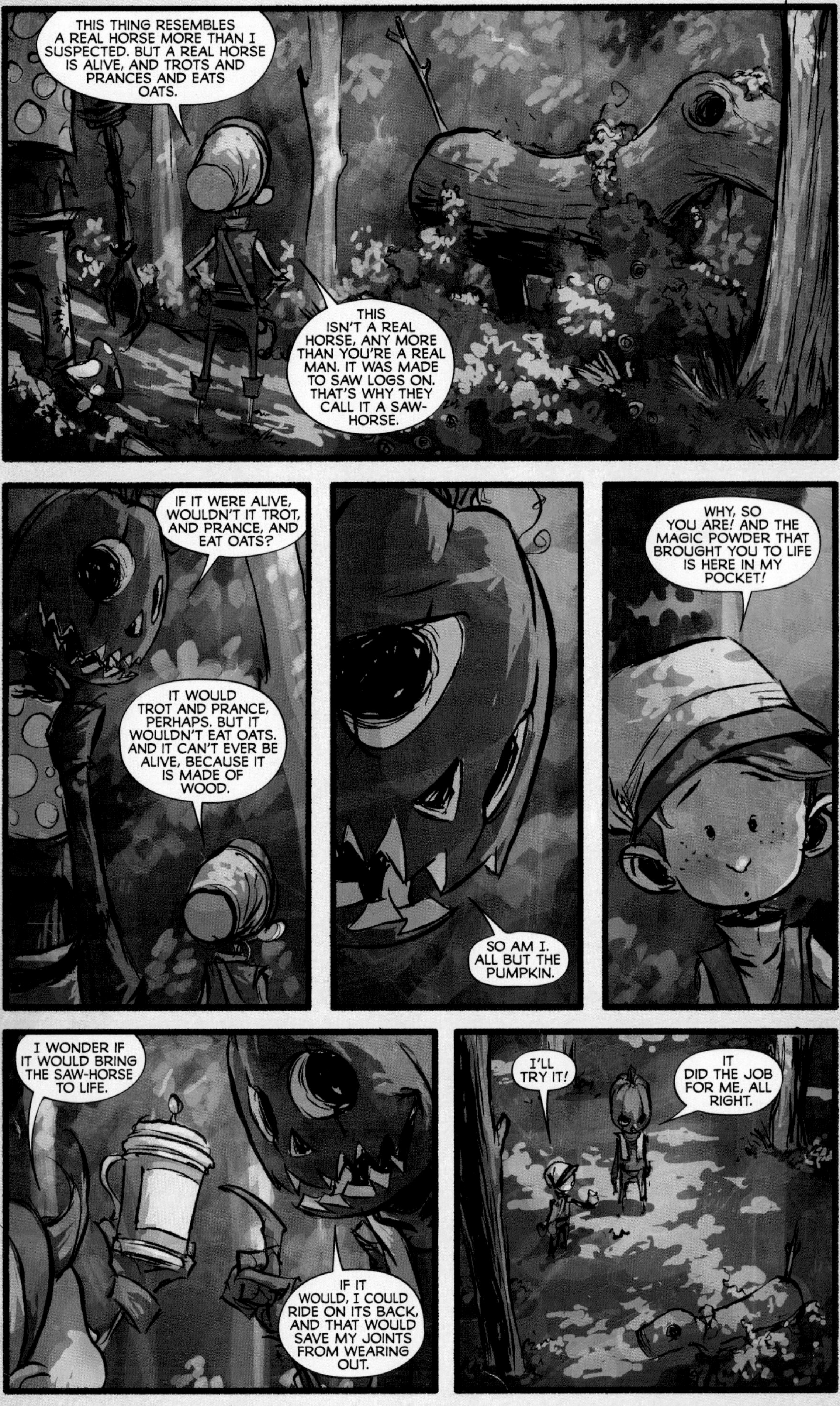
THIS THING RESEMBLES A REAL HORSE MORE THAN I SUSPECTED. BUT A REAL HORSE IS ALIVE, AND TROTS AND PRANCES AND EATS OATS.
THIS ISN'T A REAL HORSE, ANY MORE THAN YOU'RE A REAL MAN. IT WAS MADE TO SAW LOGS ON. THAT'S WHY THEY CALL IT A SAW-HORSE.
IF IT WERE ALIVE, WOULDN'T IT TROT, AND PRANCE, AND EAT OATS?
IT WOULD TROT AND PRANCE, PERHAPS. BUT IT WOULDN'T EAT OATS. AND IT CAN'T EVER BE ALIVE, BECAUSE IT IS MADE OF WOOD.
SO AM I. ALL BUT THE PUMPKIN.
WHY, SO YOU ARE! AND THE MAGIC POWDER THAT BROUGHT YOU TO LIFE IS HERE IN MY POCKET!
I WONDER IF IT WOULD BRING THE SAW-HORSE TO LIFE.
IF IT WOULD, I COULD RIDE ON ITS BACK, AND THAT WOULD SAVE MY JOINTS FROM WEARING OUT.
I'LL TRY IT!
IT DID THE JOB FOR ME, ALL RIGHT.